BuzzPop

An imprint of Little Bee Books, Inc.
251 Park Avenue South, New York, NY 10010
Copyright © 2018 by Egmont UK Limited
This BuzzPop edition, 2019

Manufactured in China HH 0419
First U.S. Edition
1 2 3 4 5 6 7 8 9 10
ISBN 978-1-4998-0987-9

buzzpopbooks.com

The Ultimate
UNICORN
JOKE BOOK

BuzzPop

YOO-HOO-nicorn!

I'm Sparkly Jim—the FUNNIEST unicorn in the magical forest (FACT). I want to welcome you to my glittery rainbow realm to hear my favorite jokes and meet all of my magical friends.

Now it's time for the MANE event. . . .
So sit back, put up your hooves, and get ready to laugh yourself HOARSE!

(Any jokes that don't make you laugh were probably written by wizards.)

Which unicorn lives
in space?

The moon-icorn.

What did the mirror
say to the unicorn?

I see you-nicorn!

Knock, knock!

Who's there?

U.

U who?

Unicorn!

Knock, knock!

Who's there?

The interrupting unicorn.

The interr-

Neigh!

Who is the smelliest unicorn?

The poo-nicorn.

Which unicorn sleeps until midday?

The noon-icorn.

Which unicorn
loves singing?

The tune-icorn.

Which unicorn helps you eat cereal?

The spoon-icorn.

What did the unicorn say to the love of his life?

Will you mare-y me?

Which unicorn
always gets
forgotten?

The who-nicorn?

Which unicorn
carries passengers
and runs on tracks?

The choo-choo-nicorn.

Which unicorn
has a cold?

The achoo-nicorn.

Which unicorn can see
into the future?

The fortun-icorn teller.

Which unicorn
causes a fuss?

The hullabaloo-nicorn.

Which unicorn is
a cat in disguise?

The mew-nicorn.

What do you say
to a really cool
unicorn?

You're a legend!

What do you
call a unicorn
without a horn?

Pointless.

What do you call
a baby unicorn?

The brand new-nicorn.

What do you call a really
scary unicorn?

A night-mare!

Why did the unicorn
cross the road?

To visit her neigh-bor.

Why are unicorns so healthy?

They eat stable diets.

Why did the unicorn sneeze?

He had hay fever.

How do
unicorns get around
the magical forest?

On uni-cycles.

What happens when you interrupt a unicorn reading the newspaper?

I don't know exactly, but there'll be some cross-words!

Where do sick unicorns go?

The horse-pital.

Why was the unicorn hanging out with a lion, a witch, and a wardrobe?

Narnia business!

Did you hear about the unicorn who made a belt out of watches?

It was a waist of time.

What do unicorns wear on their feet?

Horseshoe-nicorns.

Why was the unicorn such a good guitar player?

She knew all the uni-chords.

What did the unicorn say when he fell over?

Help—I can't giddy up!

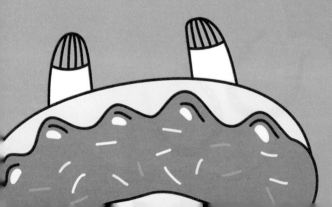

Why couldn't the Shetland unicorn pay for his shopping?

He was a bit short.

What do unicorns say when they kiss?

Ouch!

What do unicorns
like to bake?

Uni-corn muffins.

Where did the unicorns go on vacation?

To Horsta Rica.

How did they get there?

They flew-nicorn!

Why do unicorn cars win all the races?

They've got so much horse-power.

What happened to
the tiny unicorn?

He grew-nicorn.

Why aren't
unicorns funny?

Their jokes are so uni-corny!

Why was the
unicorn arrested?

She was the mane suspect.

Why can't you take
unicorns to the library?

They might use their horns!

What do unicorns
say when they watch the
Star Wars movies?

*May the horse
be with you!*

How do I
know that unicorn
spit is glittery?

*I got it straight from the horse's
mouth.*

Did you hear about the unicorn who won the marathon?

It was a one-horse race.

What do unicorns wear to school?

Uni-forms.

What is a unicorn's favorite subject in school?

Horse-tory.

What do you say to unicorns when they graduate?

Corn-gratulations!

What is a unicorn's favorite type of story?

Fairy tails.

What did the teacher say to the naughty unicorn?

Stop horsing around!

Why did the unicorn get detention?

She used foal language.

Why did the wizard do well at school?

He was so good at spelling.

Which part did the
unicorn want in
the school play?

The mane role.

How did the unicorn feel
when the gym teacher told
him to stop heading the ball?

Deflated.

Why was the
unicorn the star player
of the school's soccer team?

*She was good at hoofing the
ball up the field.*

What do unicorns
like to play in gym class?

Stable tennis.

Why did
the unicorn get a
penalty?

There was a foal.

What do
unicorns wear to
dinner parties?

Rain-bow ties.

What did the
unicorn say when
she smelled a rainbow?

Hoof-arted?

Why was the
team disappointed to
come in second place?

They wanted to whinny!

Why couldn't the unicorn tie his bow?

It was a rain-bow.

What do unicorn pirates sail in?

Rain-boats.

Which rainbow is like a massive dog?

The Great Dane-bow.

Which rainbow thinks a lot of itself?

The vain-bow.

Which rainbow appears above farms?

The grain-bow.

Which rainbow takes
everyone on vacation?

The airplane-bow.

Which rainbow is good at building?

The crane-bow.

Why were the unicorns multicolored and dripping wet?

It was pouring rain-bows.

What did the unicorn horn say to the scarf?

You stay there. I'll go on a head.

What is a unicorn's
favorite hair style?

A pony-tail.

Where do unicorns go to
ride the merry-go-round?

The unicorn-ival.

What do you get when
you cross a unicorn
and a werewolf?

A corn dog.

What is a unicorn's
signature dance move?

The Nae Nae.

What does the unicorn
call her dad?

Pop-corn.

Did you hear about
the unicorn with a
negative attitude?

She always says neigh.

What card game do unicorns play?

Uno.

Who is a unicorn's favorite member of One Direction?

Niall Horsan.

How do unicorns amp up the party?

With the neigh-dio.

What is a unicorn's favorite band?

Fifth Harmo-neigh.

Why was the unicorn floor dirty?

She never took off her horse-shoes.

What is a unicorn's favorite thing to watch on TV?

Cartoon-icorns.

What is a unicorn's favorite *Star Wars* movie?

The Horse Awakens.

And who is their favorite *Star Wars* character?

Princess Neigha.

First unicorn:
What do you think of
the magical forest?

Second unicorn:
It's oak-ay.

Why did the unicorn leave
the magical forest?

He wanted to branch out.

How do unicorns
get on the Wi-Fi in the
magical forest?

They log on.

First unicorn: I've heard
there are talking trees in
the magical forest.

Second unicorn:
I don't be-leaf you!

How do you play
magical forest
hide-and-seek?

*Close your eyes and
count to tree.*

Why didn't the
unicorn win the game
of magical forest
hide-and-seek?

He was stumped.

What do you use
to sew in the
magical forest?

Magical pine needles.

Why was the
unicorn mad at
the tree in the
magical forest?

*The tree was
throwing shade.*

Did you hear
about the unicorn
who ran into a tree in
the magical forest?

Face-palm!

What was the magical
forest party like?

Tree-mendous.

What do you call a
three-sported race in
the magical forest?

A tree-athlon.

Why were the trees the last ones to leave the magical forest party?

They wooden go.

Did you hear about the tree that vanished in the magical forest?

It was a mys-tree!

First unicorn: How was the magical forest sleepover?

Second unicorn: I slept like a log!

What kind of music do unicorns play in the magical forest?

Tree house music.

Why couldn't the sapling leave the magical forest?

It was grounded.

What is
the difference between
a bunch of carrots and a unicorn?

*One is a bunny feast and the other
is a funny beast.*

What do unicorns call a small scoop of ice cream?

A uni-cone.

What do unicorns have for breakfast?

Uni-corn flakes.

A unicorn walks into the Rainbow Sparkle Café.

The owner says, "Hey, why the long face?"

How did the unicorn
like her pasta cooked?

Al dent-neigh.

What is
a unicorn's
favorite food?

Baked pony-tatos.

What is the most
mythical vegetable?

The uni-corn.

What is good
advice at a unicorn picnic?

*Don't bite off more than
unicorn chew.*

What kind
of water do
unicorns like?

Sparkling.

What do unicorns eat at the movie theater?

Uni-popcorn.

What did the unicorn say when someone tried to take her lunch?

Hay!

What did the corn seller say to the unicorn?

U need corn?

Did you hear
about the unicorn who
tried to eat a clock?

It was time-consuming.

Two unicorns were
at a magical forest BBQ.

First unicorn: I prefer the
sparkly moon rock burger to
the rainbow burger.

Second unicorn:
Yes, it's a little meteor.

I had dinner with a
time-traveling unicorn
the other night.

*He went back
four seconds.*

Why didn't the unicorns go in the pool at the magical forest BBQ?

You shouldn't swim on a foal stomach.

What else did the unicorns eat at the magical forest BBQ?

Uni-corn on the cob.

Have you met the unicorn baker?

She's a thorough-bread.

Have you met the vegetarian unicorn?

No, I haven't met herbivore.

Why did the unicorn tell jokes to the cheese?

It was bleu.

The unicorn knew it was wrong to steal from the kitchen. So why did she do it?

It was a whisk she was willing to take.

What did the greedy little unicorn say to her friends when she wanted a midnight snack?

Hoof-eels hungry?

What did the greedy little unicorn say while eating the midnight snack?

Hoof-inished the cookies?

What did the greedy little unicorn's dad say when he found them?

It's past-ure bedtime.

What did the mermaid say when the unicorn came over to her house?

Come on in, the water's fine!

Did you hear
about the mermaid
who lies all the time?

*She's always
telling tails.*

What did
the mermaid do
for her birthday?

She had a shell-ebration.

How did the
mermaid party go?

It went swimmingly.

Did you hear about the grumpy mermaid?

She's very antiso-shell.

Did you hear about the musical mermaid?

She is very good at scales.

When do mermaid spies complete their missions?

When the coast is clear.

Why did the mermaid call the police?

It was an emergen-sea.

Where do fancy mermaids live?

In sandcastles.

Where do mermaids keep their money?

In the river-bank.

What was the wizard doing in the magical forest?

Just wand-ering around.

What did the mermaid bring to the magic picnic?

Sea-nut butter cookies.

What did
the wizard bring to
the magic picnic?

Sand-witches.

What do
I do when a
mermaid steals
my beach snack?

I scream.

Did you hear
about the witch who
made her whole left
side disappear?

She's all right now.

Did you hear
about the witch who
stole a tractor?

She turned into a field.

Who did
the witch live with?

Her broom-mate.

What did the
unicorn say when the wizard
tried to trick him?

*You won't make a foal
out of me!*

Why did the
pixie keep pulling
on the unicorn's
tail?

He got a kick out of it.

Why did the unicorn lumberjack chop down trees?

He believed he was doing random axe of kindness.

Which unicorn is a ghost in disguise?

The ooOooOoo-nicorn.

Which unicorn
is a cow in disguise?

The moo-nicorn.

At the magical forest costume party, all the dolphins dressed up as unicorns.

It was fin-tastic.

Did you hear about the T. rex who pretended to be a unicorn?

He stuck out like a saur thumb.

At the magical forest costume party, all the dogs dressed up as unicorns.

It was paw-some.

At the magical fores
costume party, all th
frogs dressed up as
unicorns.

*It was toad-ally
awesome.*

At the magical
forest costume party,
all the tortoises dressed up
as unicorns.

*It was a turtle
surprise!*

Unicorn:
Did you enjoy the jokes?

Wizard:
I thought they were wand-erful,
especially the ones I wrote!

Unicorn:
Me, too. I laughed
myself hoarse!